JEWEL OF THE AISLE: A NOVELLA

An Annabelle Archer Wedding Planner Mystery #18

LAURA DURHAM

Broadmoor Books

CHAPTER ONE

I peered through the high gate at the coral-and-white exterior of the Graycliff Hotel, stone steps sweeping up to the colonial mansion's two-story veranda with thin columns and tall windows framed with whitewashed shutters. Palm trees soared into the blue sky above, and fuchsia bougainvillea spilled over ornate wrought iron adorning the top of the stone wall surrounding the historic property. I breathed in the warm air and the scent of plumeria.

"It must be a thousand degrees," my best friend Richard said from behind me, as he walked up and hoisted his Prada carry-on bag over his shoulder. Even though it was steamy, his dark hair was immaculate and his blue, polished cotton button-down shirt unwrinkled.

I touched the damp tendrils of auburn hair escaping from my ponytail at the nape of my neck, glancing down at my rumpled, yellow sundress and wondering how he'd stayed so pristine on two flights and two taxi rides, while I looked like I'd rolled the entire way. "Well, it is the Bahamas."

"Why did Darla Douglas have to renew her vows in another country? What's wrong with Washington, DC?"

I shrugged, shifting my own less glamorous carry-on bag in my hand. "June in DC is almost as hot and muggy but without the tropical vibe."

"I've never understood vow renewals that are as extravagant as first weddings. Didn't Darla get the wedding bug out of her system when her daughter got married?"

"Apparently, planning that wedding made her want to throw herself a big bash. Mr. Douglas didn't make his money until well into their marriage, so their wedding was modest."

"A lot of fuss for nothing, if you ask me," Richard muttered as we passed through the gate and made our way through the lush greenery of the front garden and up the steps to the principal building. "If I were her, I would upgrade my diamond ring by a couple of carats and call it a day."

I didn't completely agree with him. I loved destination weddings, although I'd concede that it was a lot of travel for one weekend. Unfortunately, as one of the top wedding planners in Washington, DC, I had little more than a weekend to spare during our busy season. My other Wedding Belles brides wouldn't be thrilled if I was away for more than a couple of days.

Still, it was nice to get away from the pressure cooker atmosphere of the capitol city and embrace the laid back

Caribbean lifestyle. Even if it was only for a weekend and despite Richard not being onboard with the idea of slowing down and relaxing our expectations.

"Humpf." Richard paused when we reached the front veranda, the wood floorboards shiny. "No bellmen. I suppose we can add 'pack mule' to our job description."

I glanced at the single carry-on bags we each held. Considering the number of duffels, garment bags, and purses piled on me by bridesmaids over the years, one bag was hardly noticeable.

"If it's too taxing for you, I can always carry both bags," I drawled.

He let out a relieved breath, hooking his bag over my shoulder. "You're a dear, Annabelle." He bustled through the front door. "I'll go check us in."

So much for sarcasm.

My sandals tapped on the hardwood floors as I followed him, and I blinked as my eyes adjusted to the lower light and the dark furnishings. A crystal chandelier hung above us but was not illuminated during the day, and a navy-blue Persian carpet muffled our footsteps.

From what I'd read about the hotel, it was nearly three hundred years old, had been built by a pirate, and had been a hotspot for smuggling booze during Prohibition. It seemed slightly Old World and stuffy for the Douglas family, but they did love a good cocktail.

Richard looked around the empty foyer and toward the mahogany staircase. "This doesn't look like a lobby."

I dropped both bags on the floor, nudged them over to the wall, and pulled out my phone. "Let me ping Kate and see where everyone is."

My assistant Kate had flown down a day earlier along with our go-to florists, Buster and Mack, and hairstylist to the rich and infamous, Fern. Richard and I had stayed behind to meet with a high-touch client getting married at the end of the month. She lived in Hong Kong and had only been able to fly in on a particular day, so we'd re-booked our flights and sent our team ahead.

I wasn't worried, since the Douglas vow renewal cere-mony wasn't until late in the afternoon, and we'd finalized every detail at the walk-through months earlier, but cutting anything so close made me nervous. I reminded myself for the tenth time in the past hour that everyone on my team was a total professional.

"There you are!"

I glanced up to see Kate's blond bob poking down from the staircase, followed by her long, bare legs and a pink slip of a dress. Our usual wedding day attire was a classic black dress, but that made little sense in the Bahamas in June. The thought of wearing black made a bead of sweat trickle down my back.

"Did you forget to pack the rest of your dress, darling?" Richard asked, eyeing her as she came down the stairs in her high heel mules.

"Funny." She gave him a look, then turned her atten-tion to me. "Everyone's upstairs in the getting ready suite, aka Darla's suite."

"How's the...?" I faltered on the word "bride" because technically our bride for the day was Darla Douglas, who we'd known as the mother of the bride for her daughter's wedding and mother of the groom for her son's. It was strange to think of her as our bride, even though she was the one renewing her vows and wearing the white dress.

Kate grinned at me. "It's weird, right? I can't wrap my mind around Darla not being the mother of the bride today. But she's great." She lowered her voice. "The champagne hasn't hurt."

No surprise there. Darla Douglas and her daughter Debbie were some of our favorite clients because they had hired us so often, had big budgets, and stayed in a state of perpetual happy hour. I would consider the preppy pair ladies who lunched—if the lunches were liquid and lasted most of the day. They'd even been known to carry monogrammed cocktail shakers in their purses, their version of being prepared for any emergency.

"I assume Fern is with them?" I asked, putting a hand on Kate's arm. "Please tell me he's doing their hair sober."

Kate hesitated, which spoke volumes. "What I can tell you is that I've kept him from doing Darla's hair in a sideswept bouffant."

"I don't even know what that is," I said. Whatever it was, I couldn't imagine the middle aged brunette who wore Burberry headbands pulling it off. Although Fern with a few drinks in him was fun, it meant big hair.

"I'm hoping to use pictures from this in some upcoming promotional pieces, so absolutely no State Fair hair," Richard said, leveling a finger at Kate, as if she was the one wielding the brush and hairspray.

She held both palms up. "You don't have to convince me. Once the buzz wears off, most brides aren't thrilled they walked down the aisle with a beehive."

"The good news is that Darla doesn't have enough hair for a true updo," I said.

Kate gave me a wicked smile. "But Caroline does."

"Caroline?" Now I understood the smile. Darla's daughter-in-law was the definition of an icy blond in every way, and I'd forgotten that she was one of the bridesmaids. I doubted even Fern could sweet-talk her into big hair.

Richard cringed. "The bride whose wedding flowers were cacti?"

"Only on the dining tables," I said, remembering the Christmas wedding that had been the opposite of jolly, "but yes."

"Another reason I'm glad I'm the caterer and not the planner." Richard fluttered a hand at us. "While you wrangle Fern and the ladies, I'm going to check on the reception set-up." He gazed in the direction of the restaurant at the back of the hotel. "They'd better be using the to-the-floor linens we had shipped down. If I see a table leg, I will lose my mind."

As one of DC's most exclusive caterers, Richard had done all the Douglas events for years. It had been unthinkable that they would have a party without him, so he'd been flown down as the catering consultant. I wasn't sure how happy the Graycliff restaurant was about this, especially since he'd deemed most of their linens and china unsatisfactory, but I was grateful to have one more thing taken off my plate.

"Perfect." I held up my phone and waved it. "Text me if you need anything."

"Don't worry about me, darling. This place is about to move from island time to Richard time."

I stifled a groan. DC precision was not something that translated well to a tropical island, which was why we'd brought most of our vendors with us. "Good luck."

Richard arched an eyebrow as he spun on his heel. "Luck has nothing to do with it."

CHAPTER TWO

"The kitchen staff's day is about to get a lot more interesting," Kate muttered as she watched Richard walk away.

I made a mental note to check on the kitchen later to ensure there wasn't a mass walk-out, then I turned to Kate. "Now that Richard's gone, give it to me straight. How are things really going?"

She grinned at me. "Honestly? Better than you'd imagine, considering that rum punch seems to be on tap around here."

"Maybe that's why. It only seems like everything is okay, but everyone is soused."

Kate shrugged. "The bride is happy, the skies are clear, and no one's been murdered. For us, I'd call it a success."

She had a point.

"Let's go." Kate pivoted and started back up the stairs. "Darla's been asking about you all morning."

I grabbed my overnight bag and followed Kate up the stairs to a wooden door with an oval nameplate that read

"Jasmine." Before she could push open the door, a tall, dark-haired man stepped out, almost walking into us.

"Pardon me." He seemed startled to see us, and it took me a few moments to recognize Mr. Douglas, the father of the bride and today's groom. I knew him primarily as the person who signed the checks, but he'd always been generous with smiles and tips, making him one of my favorite fathers of the bride.

"Hi, Mr. Douglas," I said. "How's it going in there?"

He blinked at me for a moment—perhaps trying to place me, since he only ever saw me at busy family weddings wearing black and carrying a schedule—then grinned. "So far, so good." He patted my arm as he sidled between Kate and me. "I'm off to get ready myself."

I didn't need to check my watch to know that he didn't need to get dressed so early, but I always appreciated anyone who was ahead of schedule. "We'll pop by later to pin on your boutonnière."

He gave me another charming smile and pat on the arm. I watched him walk off, thinking that he made a more nervous groom than he did a father of the bride. But I supposed it was always more nerve-wracking being the one getting married, even if it was a vow renewal.

Kate tugged my arm, pulling me into the Jasmine suite. Stepping inside after her, I was surprised to find the suite much lighter and airier than the downstairs. The walls were pale green with light streaming in from high windows and French doors that led outside to the second-floor wraparound veranda. A large living room with cream-colored carpeting had a built-in bar on one end, as well as a small dining table and sofa grouping. Louis

Vuitton duffel bags and totes lay open on the floor, and it appeared that some of their contents was scattered throughout the room.

"Annabelle!" Fern waved from where he stood next to the open French doors, his hair products covering the dining table and a dark-haired woman on the stool in front of him. She wore a hot-pink silk robe and faced away from me. I couldn't tell if it was Debbie or Darla, but my eyes mostly focused on Fern.

His dark hair was swept back into a low ponytail with not a hair out of place. He wore white pants, but over that he had on a tunic that reached below his knees decorated in orange and turquoise patterns.

Before I could open my mouth, Kate whispered, "It's what they wear in traditional Junkanoo parades here. He got it in a specialty store."

I didn't know what a Junkanoo parade was, but I did know that Fern always dressed for the occasion. Whether that meant donning the wedding colors, wearing a seersucker suit and straw boater hat for a garden party, or even a sari to an Indian wedding, he tailored his outfit to the celebration. It was the opposite of me wearing a black dress as my wedding day uniform, but he could pull it off. If I showed up dressed as a geisha for an Asian wedding, I'd probably be fired.

"Is that Annabelle?" The woman in the chair swiveled her head. I saw that it was Darla, the former mother of the bride and current bride.

I dropped my overnight bag by the door and crossed to her. "How's our bride today?"

She giggled and hiccupped. "Can you believe I'm a bride again? After thirty years?"

I noticed the glass of champagne in her hand. "I think it's great that you're renewing your vows. It's about time you had a party after all the weddings, engagement parties, and showers you've thrown."

Her eyes were slightly unfocused as she reached for my hand. "You know our first wedding was tiny. Nothing like the weddings I threw for Debbie and Carlton. Now it's my turn."

Fern leaned down close to her ear. "That's why we have to make you look fabulous, sweetie."

I locked eyes with him. "No eighties hair."

He inhaled sharply. "You wound me."

I cut my gaze to his can of industrial strength hair spray, and his already pink cheeks reddened.

"Fine." He let out a sigh. "But feathering is coming back in, you know."

"Not by today it's not." I glanced over at the French doors leading into the bedroom and saw a sleigh bed with a dress laid out across the floral duvet, along with a veil and a couple of black velvet jewelry boxes.

There was a commotion behind me, and I twisted to see lots of black leather and brightly colored flowers proceeding through the doorway. Behind that, a waiter wheeled in a room service cart with an ice bucket of Champagne and a pair of silver domed plates.

"I come bearing bouquets." Mack peeked his bald head over the flowers, and I saw a flash of his dark red goatee.

"Flowers?" Debbie, the bride's daughter and our former bride, appeared from the bedroom, also wearing a pink silk robe with her brown hair in curlers. "Oh, hi, Annabelle!"

Mack made his way toward us, his black leather pants crinkling as he walked. He was one half of the Harley-riding, leather-wearing floral duo we'd brought down from DC. If he and his partner Buster looked out of place in the Washington floral world with their piercings and tattoos, they really didn't blend in the Bahamas. As if conceding to the tropical environment, Mack had ditched his usual black leather jacket for a leather vest emblazoned with a "Road Riders for Jesus" patch. Even so, I imagined it was incredibly hot.

"I saw Richard," Mack said with a grin. "He's downstairs with Buster. He said your flight was harrowing."

"It was fine. Richard thinks all flights in small planes are harrowing."

He laughed and held the long white box at eye level. I counted the one ivory bouquet for Darla and two hot pink, orange, and yellow attendant bouquets, breathing in the sweet perfume of the blooms.

"They're gorgeous." Debbie clapped her hands as she beamed at Mack. "Not that we expected anything less."

Mack blushed from the compliment, his cheeks almost matching his goatee.

"How's Caroline?" I asked Debbie, since I hadn't spotted the blonde. I knew Debbie wasn't close to her sister-in-law, but I also knew that Darla hadn't wanted to exclude the woman from being in the ceremony.

Debbie opened her mouth to answer, but the room service waiter rolled the cart beside us. "Where would you like the champagne?"

"In here!" A sharp voice I instantly recognized as belonging to Caroline Douglas called out from inside the bedroom, more of an order than a request.

"We're doing our nails in the bathroom," Debbie explained with a wink to me. "I thought we could use some more bubbly."

I wasn't sure if there was enough champagne in the world to relax Caroline, but I had to give Debbie credit for trying. Her brother's wife was almost the opposite of the petite, bubbly Douglas women. She was tall and willowy with long, straight, blond hair. She wore only black and nothing remotely girly. Planning her December wedding the year before had been a challenge, since the woman thought Christmas decor was "too cheery." Hence the cacti.

"They're perfect," I told Mack. "Why don't we put the box on the bed?"

He followed the wheeling room service cart through the French doors while I glanced at my phone and turned back to Darla. "We're doing great on time. You're even ahead of schedule."

"Oh, Annabelle," Fern said in what I'm sure he thought was a Bahamian accent. "We're on island time now."

The waiter passed me, coming from the bedroom, this time without the rolling cart. Mack was close on his heels, giving me a small wave as he lumbered from the suite. Before he could close the door, another man knocked while stepping inside. Tall and wearing a dark suit, he held out a shiny gold box tied with an aquamarine ribbon.

"A gift from the Graycliff," he said with a smile.

Darla's eyes widened. "Are those the famous Graycliff

chocolates? These are so good. We did a tour of the chocolatier and got a sampling yesterday."

She waved the man over and eagerly unwrapped the box while Fern teased her hair. "I know I shouldn't, but it is my wedding day. One of them, anyway." She plucked a truffle from the box and bit into it, closing her eyes as she chewed.

"Did I hear the word chocolate?" Debbie called from the bathroom.

Darla beamed at the man. "Do you mind terribly walking them to her?"

His smile didn't falter, but I wondered if he'd imagined he'd be a roving chocolate butler when he'd been sent up to deliver the gift.

I used the momentary excitement over the chocolates to pull Kate off to the side. "How did it go with the minister yesterday?"

"Easy peasy." She stepped out of her shoes and instantly shrunk a few inches. "Since it's a vow renewal, we didn't need a license, so I gave the guy the readings and that was that. He'll be here an hour before the ceremony."

I mentally crossed another thing off my list as the man who'd delivered the chocolates emerged from the bedroom, put the opened box on the coffee table, and left the suite. "I'm assuming the dad has the rings. We can get them from him when we pin on his boutonnière later."

"Actually…" Kate started to say.

"The rings are in the bedroom," Darla called out, obviously overhearing our conversation. "Have I not shown you the new three-carat diamond Robert got for me?"

It seemed that Darla was getting her second wedding and a diamond upgrade. Richard would be pleased.

Darla didn't wait for me to answer before waving an arm in the direction of the bedroom. "Debbie, honey! Bring me the ring box. I want to show Annabelle."

After a few moments of shuffling, Debbie rushed from the bedroom, her cheeks pale. "The ring is gone!"

CHAPTER THREE

"Debbie swears the ring was in the box when she put it out on the bed," I told Richard once we'd calmed everyone down and gotten the getting ready process back on track. He'd come upstairs after noticing a commotion with the hotel staff and hearing that a theft of a diamond ring had been reported. It hadn't taken him long to figure out it was our client's ring that had disappeared.

"How sober was she when she put out the box?" One of his perfectly groomed brows arched as we stood outside the Jasmine suite talking in lowered voices.

I tried to give him a severe look, but I knew he was right. Debbie and Darla were almost always a few cocktails ahead of the rest of the crowd. "She wouldn't make a mistake when it comes to jewelry. Besides, Darla claims the ring box went straight from her purse to the bed and that she'd peeked at the diamond again before handing it to Debbie."

"Then it must have been swiped by someone who

came in the suite after that." He pressed a hand to his heart. "Thank heavens I'm in the clear for once. I've had enough of being wrongly accused of crimes, thank you very much."

I was going to say that it hadn't happened so many times, but I knew from experience that being falsely accused even once was one time too many. And to be fair, Richard had been a suspect in more than one murder investigation. "You're in the clear. And so am I, since I barely walked into the suite before the ring went missing and never even set foot in the bedroom."

"Might I point out that we've been on the island for less than an hour, and we're already embroiled in a criminal investigation?"

I sighed. "Your point?"

He folded his arms over his chest. "My point, darling, is that I would love a break from chasing murders and hunting down crooks."

"You and me both." My voice went up an octave. "It's not like I want to add solving crimes to my wedding day to-do list."

He twitched one shoulder up and down. "I'm only saying you seem to be a crime magnet."

"Maybe it's not me. Maybe it's you. After all, you're always with me."

He opened his mouth to protest, then clamped it shut.

"I suggest we solve this thing as quickly as possible before word gets out," I said, before my best friend could come up with a clever retort.

Richard still looked affronted by my suggestion that he was the crime magnet, but he gave an almost imperceptible nod. "Fine. There should be a small window of time the ring could have been taken and an even smaller number of people with access to that bed."

I tapped a finger on my chin. "Actually, it was a little chaotic for a while there. The flowers were delivered and put on the bed, a room service waiter wheeled a cart into the bathroom through the bedroom, and another hotel staff member delivered Graycliff chocolates. That was only during the five minutes I was inside."

"Sounds like Grand Central," Richard muttered as we both stepped aside for another room service cart—this one with more bottles of champagne—to be wheeled into the room. "And no one saw anything?"

I thought back to all the movement and shook my head. "I didn't notice anything, but I was also distracted by the bride and talking about the schedule with Kate."

"You did say the flowers were delivered. Why don't we talk to our boys in black? Maybe they were paying more attention than some people."

I ignored his pointed comment and headed for the staircase, hurrying down to the first floor.

"The last I saw Buster and Mack, they were in the restaurant." Richard pointed to the back of the building, and I followed him through a rather fussy parlor and into a long narrow room lined with floor to ceiling windows overlooking lots of lush tropical greenery. Round tables filled the space and were draped with white cloths. At the far end, Buster adjusted a brightly colored floral arrangement in the center of one of the tables.

Like Mack, he was over six feet tall and could be graciously called husky, with black leather covering most of his bulky frame. He wore motorcycle goggles perched on top of his bald head and had a dark brown goatee.

He glanced up at the tapping of our feet on the hardwood floor, his wide smile fading when he saw our expressions. "What's wrong? Do they hate the flowers?"

"Of course not," I said, weaving my way through the tables toward him, the heady scent of the fresh blooms tickling my nose.

"Because it is not easy finding every kind of flower down here," he said. "If you don't love tropicals, you're in trouble."

"The flowers are perfect," I reassured him, putting a hand on his thick, tattooed forearm. "Did Mack come back down?"

Buster tilted his head at me. "He stepped out to call Prue." His voice caught in his throat. "It's hard to be away from Merry, especially now that she's walking everywhere." He pulled his phone from his pants pocket. "Did I show you the videos?"

As much as I adored the baby that Buster and Mack had become surrogate fathers for, I didn't have time to watch more videos of the little girl taking tentative steps around their flower shop. Behind me, Richard made an impatient noise. No surprise, since he was not a baby person, even though he was begrudgingly fond of Merry.

"You must be out of your mind if you think I'm going to watch one more—" he began to say, but I elbowed him sharply in the ribs.

"There he is!" Buster's gaze shifted over my head, and I heard the familiar creak of leather being strained to its breaking point.

I pivoted to see Mack approaching, his phone in one hand and a big grin on his face.

"Everything's fine," he said. "They miss us, of course, but I promised we'd bring back presents. What do you think a one-and-a-half-year-old would like from the Bahamas?"

"Oh, for heaven's sake," Richard muttered under his breath.

I shot him a look. "Don't tell me you're not getting your dog a present because I know you."

His cheeks colored, and he muttered something about Hermès looking dapper in straw hats and tropical colors. Despite also not being a pet person, Richard was obsessed with his significant other's Yorkie, whom he'd named Hermès and had taken to carrying with him in his man bag. They even had matching designer outfits, which meant he had no room to complain about the two floral designers being indulgent.

I turned my attention back to Mack. "When you dropped off the flowers upstairs, do you remember seeing a ring box on the bed?"

His brow furrowed. "Maybe. I honestly didn't focus too much on the things laid out on the bed, aside from trying to avoid them. Why?"

"Darla's ring is missing."

Mack looked even more confused. "The one she wears?"

I shook my head. "Her husband bought her a big new diamond ring for their vow renewal. It was in a ring box on the bed so the photographer could take photos of it on the veil and with the other wedding accessories. Now it's gone."

Mack slapped a hand over his mouth. "And you think I...?"

"Of course not," I insisted even as Richard hemmed and hawed. "We thought you might have seen something that could help us track it down."

He dropped his hand from his mouth and his shoulders relaxed. "I wish I had. I left pretty quickly because there wasn't room in there for the room service trolley and me."

I snapped my fingers. "That's right. The waiter was in and out of the bedroom at the same time. You didn't happen to see him near the ring box, did you?"

"No, but I did leave him in the bedroom to show Debbie and Caroline the bouquets. The room service trolley wouldn't fit in the bathroom, so he left it in the bedroom against one of the walls while I presented the flowers to the ladies."

"What did they think?" Buster asked.

"About the flowers? Debbie loved them, and Caroline didn't make a face." Mack rolled his eyes, and I couldn't help joining him in grinning. After working on the daughter-in-law's wedding, we were all aware of her lack of enthusiasm for just about anything.

Richard cleared his throat. "Back to the matter at hand, people. It would only take a few seconds to pocket a ring."

"If you want to talk to the waiter who left the suite with me, I saw him heading out the back of the hotel," Mack said.

"Was he heading to set up the pool area for the reception?" I asked.

Mack shook his head. "I don't think so. I overheard him say he was clocking out for the day."

"So, he's leaving?" Richard's brow furrowed. "As in, making a fast getaway?"

CHAPTER FOUR

"Faster, Annabelle!" Richard cried as we ran out the back of the hotel and into the garden.

I shot him a sideways glance as we hurried down the stairs shoulder-to-shoulder, glad I was wearing sensible flat sandals since the uneven paving stones around the hotel appeared to be original to the property. "We're going the same speed. I didn't exactly wear running shoes, you know. Your shoes look more like sneakers than my shoes do."

He huffed out a breath, more from impatience than exertion. "I hope you aren't referring to my Prada loafers. Honestly, darling. As if I would own an item of footwear called 'sneakers.'"

I swept aside a wide palm frond as we rushed down even more stairs. The heat and humidity were high enough to make standing outside a sticky proposition but running made beads of sweat trail down my spine and gather along my upper lip. I groaned. Just what I needed while coordinating a high-end wedding.

As we descended into the lower garden, Richard clutched my arm. "There he is!"

The young man I recognized as the waiter from earlier stood at the back gate talking with another man, both in Graycliff uniforms. Their eyes widened as we approached at a near run.

"Citizen's arrest." Richard waved a finger at the man with close-cropped black hair while he put his other hand on his side and sucked in a breath.

"What?" The man looked thoroughly confused as his gaze darted from his colleague to us.

Even if citizen arrests were a thing in the Bahamas, I doubted that random Americans could make them.

"Don't mind him," I said, attempting to give the man my most comforting smile and not gasp while doing so. "We wanted to talk to you about the delivery you made to the bridal suite earlier."

"The champagne?" He furrowed his brow. "Was there a problem with it?"

I shook my head. "As far as I know, it was fine." And knowing Darla and Debbie, the bubbly was long gone by now. "Did you hear about the missing ring?"

His eyes widened. "Ring? From that room?" He shook his head vigorously. "I wheeled in that cart and then clocked out."

Richard made a noise in his throat that indicated his doubt, but I ignored him. From my memory, the waiter had entered and exited the bedroom almost in lock step with Mack as he'd delivered the flowers. Even though

Mack had said he'd left the waiter in the bedroom briefly, it was hard to imagine how the man would have been able to open a ring box and snatch the ring without being seen by Mack or the bridesmaids.

"Did you notice a ring box on the bed when you went in?" I asked.

The man scrunched his lips to one side as he thought. "I wasn't paying attention to much except finding a good place to leave the cart that people wouldn't stumble over."

I nodded. He seemed sincere, but I didn't know anything about him He could be a skilled actor—or a talented pickpocket.

"I'm telling you; I don't know a thing about a missing ring."

"Then you won't mind coming back up to the hotel to talk to the manager," Richard said. "Or turning out your pockets."

The waiter shrugged. "Fine by me. I've got nothing to hide." He even reached into the pockets of his pants and tugged them inside out, proving they contained nothing but trace amounts of lint.

It was then that I noticed he didn't carry a bag of any kind, and there were no pockets on his uniform shirt. The same went for his colleague, who also pulled his pants pockets inside out. That left precious few places to hide a big diamond ring.

I exchanged a look with Richard, whose victorious expression had been replaced by a slightly dejected one. "I believe you, but it might be best to come back to the hotel so you can give an official statement and be cleared. That way there won't be any possibility of misunderstanding."

And if one of the men had managed to hide the ring, keeping them close would prevent them from getting it off the property. At the moment, my number one priority was recovering the ring in time for the ceremony. That, and keeping Darla and Debbie calm—and sober.

Both men agreed, and we all traipsed up the stairs through the garden, with Richard and me bringing up the rear.

"That didn't go quite like I expected," I whispered to him as I dabbed at my dewy upper lip.

"You mean because we still have no diamond ring?" Richard snapped off a nearby palm frond and started to fan himself as we walked.

"Let's look at the bright side. We prevented a witness from leaving. That's a good thing. I'd much rather chase him down here than all over the island."

"I, for one, would prefer not to include any form of foot chase on my wedding days." He fluttered the palm frond faster, stirring up a decent breeze that drifted over to me. "But that might be too much to ask from a Wedding Belles wedding."

"If it's too much for you, there are other caterers," I said, letting my words drift off.

Richard stopped fanning himself and peered over the frond. "I'm going to pretend you didn't say that."

Despite our sniping, Richard knew that he was my first choice of caterers. Not only because he'd been the only one to give me a chance when I'd started my business, but because he was the best in the city. He might be obsessive about details, but that made him outstanding at catering high-end events. It did not, however, make him go with the flow when it came to changes on the event day or unexpected criminal activity.

We walked up the rest of the way with Richard muttering darkly beside me and waving his fanned leaf with the skill of a Regency era debutante. Despite the heat and his aggressive fanning, not a drop of sweat shone on his face. How did he manage it? I was on the verge of wilting like an overcooked soufflé—or at the very least, sweating through my sundress.

We entered the back of the hotel through the glass-paned doors, and I sighed as the cool air hit me along with the scent of cut flowers.

"You found him!" Mack said as he spotted us, lowering his eyes when the waiter glanced at him. "Not that I thought—"

"We're going to make sure everyone's name is cleared before they leave," I said before Mack could talk himself into a hole. "Just to protect the hotel and staff."

Before we could make it any further inside, Kate skidded into the room, her gaze sweeping the room and landing on me.

My stomach clenched. I knew that look. "What's wrong?"

Richard dropped his palm frond, and it swirled to the floor. "Another wedding disaster?"

"More like a there's-not-going-to-be-a-wedding disaster." Kate scraped her perfectly manicured fingers through her hair. "The bride says she won't go through with it."

CHAPTER FIVE

"That's ridiculous." Richard snatched his palm frond from the floor. "This is a vow renewal. She's already married. If she doesn't go through with it, she's still married. She just doesn't get a fancy party."

Although this was technically true, I doubted my clients would consider the day a success if it didn't include an actual renewal of vows. And I'd never had a bride or groom back out of a wedding yet—at least not on the wedding day itself. It was a point of pride.

"She's upset about the ring," I said. "I get that, but we have to move forward as if we're going to recover it, which we will."

"Speaking of finding the ring," Kate shifted from one foot to the other. "Shouldn't we call the police?"

"It does feel strange not to have a police presence at a crime scene." Richard cut his eyes to me. "Although it may be stranger to have a detective on the case that Annabelle isn't personally involved with."

I opened my mouth to argue that my DC police detective husband wasn't always on our cases, but Richard was right. More often than not, we'd had the handsome Detective Reese by our sides as we'd puzzled out cases related to our weddings. It felt odd not having him poring over the clues and warning me to stay out of his case. "I assumed hotel security would call in the local authorities."

"Unless they want to handle it in-house and avoid the bad publicity," the waiter said.

I'd almost forgotten that he and the other employee were still with us, and that we'd come back up to the hotel so they could talk with security. I took a deep breath. "Okay, Kate and I will go to the bridal suite and talk the bride back into the wedding while Richard finds hotel security and gets the staff's statements." I lowered my voice to Richard. "And while you're at it, find out why the police haven't been called in."

"I suppose I don't have a choice if I want to have a dining experience to coordinate." Richard drew himself up to his full height. "I don't know what you'd do without me, Annabelle." Then he turned toward the lobby, beckoning the two hotel staff members to follow him.

"What can we do to help?" Mack asked.

"Assume that everything will proceed according to plan," I told him, sounding more confident than I felt. "Kate and I are on it."

Mack nodded and headed back to where he'd been placing floral arrangements on tables while Kate and I hurried through the deserted public areas of the hotel and up the stairs to the Jasmine suite.

"You're sure you can convince Darla to go through

with the ceremony without the ring?" Kate asked, her hand on the suite's doorknob.

"As long as everyone is on board with the plan." I took a breath to steady my nerves. "Which means we can't let Fern whip everyone up into a frenzy or get them too drunk."

"With Darla, I'm not even sure what 'too drunk' would be. I'm pretty sure I've never seen her or Debbie stone cold sober."

"And I'm guessing today isn't the day we want to dry them out." I shook my head as I thought of the mother daughter duo, who seemed to exist in a permanent state of gin-soaked euphoria. We needed them to stay happy. Or at least as happy as it was possible to be, considering that Darla's huge diamond ring had been stolen.

Kate pushed open the door to the bridal suite, and I braced myself for an onslaught of tears or even deadly quiet. I did not expect to see Fern leading the woman around the living room in a conga line.

"Annabelle! Kate!" He waved us over, the poufy sleeves of his brightly colored shirt flapping in time to the reggae music. "Join us!"

Kate and I exchanged a look, then Kate shrugged. "It's better than the alternative."

I wasn't completely sure what the alternative to a conga line was, but she had a point. At least Fern was keeping spirits high, although I doubted we were on schedule anymore.

Kate hopped in the line between Debbie and Darla, kicking her feet out as they made a winding path around the room.

"Come on, Annabelle," I muttered to myself. "It's all in the name of the job."

Then I joined the line behind Fern, who beamed at me. "That's more like it, sweetie. I told the girls that a little thing like a missing ring wouldn't ruin their day. Besides, we're going to find it."

"Of course, we are," I said. "I'm glad you're so sure."

"When have we ever failed to solve a crime?"

My cheeks warmed with pride. I wasn't thrilled that we'd had so many crimes at our weddings, but Fern was right. We'd solved each and every one of them.

I hopped from one foot to the other behind Fern, keeping a hand firmly attached to his waist while I waved the other in the air. I twisted my neck to see the bride behind me, followed by Kate, Debbie, and an older Bahamian woman in a Graycliff uniform.

"Did you rope one of the staff into dancing?" I asked Fern when I spun back around.

Fern glanced back at me, then his gaze drifted over my head. "You mean Eliana? She's not just a member of the staff, Annabelle. She's going to help us find the ring."

"We already searched the room from end to end."

"Not by searching. She's going to perform some witchcraft."

I almost tripped over my feet and then his. "Witchcraft?"

Fern lowered his voice to a stage whisper that I could still hear over the reggae music. "Technically it's called Obeah here in the Bahamas, and it's nothing like voodoo." His brow furrowed. "At least I don't think it is."

I stole a furtive glance at the curvy lady at the back of the conga line. "How is witchcraft going to find the ring?"

Fern pressed his lips together briefly. "She wasn't very specific, but she did say she could help, then this song came on, and we had to conga."

I leveled a gaze at my go-to hairdresser even as we continued to dance. I didn't hold much stock in spells or charms or woo woo stuff, but I knew the power of suggestion could be potent, and if it convinced Darla to go through with the ceremony, then I was all for it. "Do our very Protestant clients know about this plan?"

"Darla is all for it." Fern winked at me. "She thinks it's part of the Bahamian wedding experience."

"Whatever happens, I cannot have this wedding cursed, jinxed or otherwise voodoo-ed, so tread lightly, or I'll curse you myself."

Fern's eyes widened before he made a cross over his heart.

The song ended, and everyone broke apart and clapped.

"That was fun," Darla said, her cheeks flushed and her eyes bright.

"I wish we'd had a conga line at my wedding," Debbie added, "Although it wouldn't have fit the theme."

I thought of the other family wedding we'd planned, that of her brother and Caroline. There was no question that a conga line wouldn't have fit the wintery ice queen mood of that wedding. I glanced around, noting that the daughter-in-law was not there, then realized she'd probably hidden at the first mention of dancing.

I pulled out my wedding day timeline, then tugged

Kate over to one side. "I'm going to go check in with Richard. Can you make sure we stay on schedule for photos in the garden?"

Kate glanced at her phone. "No problem. Miraculously, we're still ahead of schedule."

"But my schedule didn't account for Bahamian magic to put a good omen on the wedding."

Kate looked perplexed. "What?"

I spotted Fern pulling out a dining room chair for the older Bahamian woman and Debbie and Darla sitting across from her, a collection of hair products spanning the table between them. "I'll let Fern explain everything."

CHAPTER SIX

I trudged down the stairs to the lobby, sighing.

"Don't tell me that Annabelle Archer is letting this little hiccup get the better of her."

I recognized Richard's voice, then saw him at the base of the staircase, one hand on his hip. "Hiccup? It's a three-carat diamond."

"At least it wasn't a dead body. I'll take missing jewelry over a corpse any day."

He had a point. We'd dealt with much worse.

"How's the family holding up?" he asked once I'd reached him.

"Surprisingly cheery. Of course, they've been drinking a lot, Fern has them dancing to reggae music, and now one of the maids is casting some sort of omen over the wedding."

"Talk about full-service cleaning," Richard muttered. "You'd never get an American housekeeper to do that, especially if she's union."

I elbowed him. "Why do I feel like this wedding is slowly going off the rails?"

"Darling." He put an arm around my shoulders. "Every event feels like riding a runaway horse toward a burning stable until it all comes together in the end."

"You're right. I was hoping that since this was a vow renewal and a family we've worked with before, that maybe we'd get a break, and it would be a breeze."

Richard laughed. "It was a nice thought." He eyed me. "Have you finally found a mystery you don't want to investigate."

I ignored his faux shock. "Despite what you might think, I do not relish juggling crime and brides."

"You could have fooled me."

"People hire us to solve their problems and take away their wedding stress. I can't exactly ignore crimes that impact their weddings. That would be bad for business."

"Like the corpses."

I shot him a look. "I would love to leave it all to the police, but that hasn't always worked out in the past. Since part of my job is to fix things on the wedding day, I'm not sure how I'm going to get out of trying to track down this ring."

Richard led me into the parlor with the baby grand piano. It smelled like furniture polish and old books, which was a strangely comforting combination.

"Especially with your reputation," Richard said in a hushed voice, as if I had a reputation for betting on ponies instead of solving crimes. "And your better half."

I fought the urge to roll my eyes. "I'm not calling Reese." My significant other would not be pleased I'd gotten myself embroiled in yet another crime. "Did you find out if the Bahamian police are involved yet?"

Richard frowned. "I spoke to the hotel's head of security. You were right. They want to keep the matter in-house. But he did take the waiters' statements."

"I guess that's something, but shouldn't we be calling in bigger guns? This is a valuable ring we're talking about. What do I tell the Douglas family when they ask about the police response?"

"That's the odd thing, Annabelle." Richard glanced around him, even though the room was empty. "According to the security head, it was Mr. Douglas who requested keeping the matter quiet. He didn't want to file a police report."

I shook my head. "That doesn't make any sense. If he doesn't file a police report, he won't be able to get an insurance settlement."

"Maybe it wasn't insured," Richard said.

I tilted my head at him. "Wealthy people insure everything. It's not like the Douglases are new money. This isn't their first rodeo. No way would Darla fly down with a massive diamond ring unless it was insured."

"Then explain why Mr. Douglas doesn't want the police involved."

I had no explanation that made any sense, and my head was starting to hurt. "Okay, so if the police aren't being called in, that means it's up to us to solve it."

"What about hotel security?"

"Us and hotel security." I corrected myself, although from what I'd heard, the hotel's security team consisted of one person.

Richard crossed his arms over his chest and smirked at me. "Does that mean you're over your reluctance to investigate?"

"Only because we have no choice. If we don't find the ring, the ceremony will be a no-go."

"Or at least no fun." Richard made a face. "I can only imagine the mood hanging over the event if that diamond doesn't turn up. No one will pay any attention to my menu creation."

"That would be a crime," I deadpanned.

"Exactly," Richard said, either not getting my sarcasm or ignoring it. "We'd better stop dilly dallying and solve this thing or all my—I mean our—hard work will be down the drain." He tapped his chin. "Aside from Mack delivering the flowers and the room service tray being delivered, who was near that ring box?"

"The hotel delivered chocolates, and I'm pretty sure they took them to Darla and Caroline."

Richard shuddered. "Chocolates. We should probably be grateful that our bridal party isn't keeling over."

"Not every box of chocolates is poisoned." I couldn't believe Richard was still jittery after an unfortunate incident the year before with a poisoned chocolate truffle.

"Perhaps not," he said, "but you weren't almost sent to the big house because of one."

It would be pointless to tell Richard that he was being overly dramatic, so I patted his arm and gave him what I hoped was a sympathetic nod. "Let's assume these chocolates are not poisoned and focus on the crime of the moment. The person who delivered them would have walked right by the ring box, which makes him a potential suspect."

"The front desk can tell us who delivered them." Richard took long steps toward the foyer, and I followed behind him as he approached a tall man in a dark suit at the base of the stairs.

"It's you," I said, recognizing the Bahamian man who'd delivered the box of Graycliff chocolates.

He cocked his head at us, his hand pausing over the polished wood banister. "Can I be of assistance?"

"You delivered a box of chocolates to the Jasmine suite," I said. "For the Douglas vow renewal."

He nodded. "Yes, of course. I was just on my way to meet with our security chief."

"Oh." I studied his impeccable suit. "Are you with hotel management?"

"I am the general manager of the Graycliff." His voice was serious, but held a slight island lilt.

"Convenient," Richard said, his arms folded across his chest.

I found it curious that the general manager of the hotel had delivered the gift to the suite, although it was a small hotel, and this was the Bahamas. Things definitely ran differently on the island than they would in DC.

"Did you happen to notice a black ring box on the bed when you took the chocolates in to the bathroom?" I asked.

One eyebrow curved upward. "I do not remember one, but then again, I only passed through the room briefly."

I nodded. I hadn't recalled him spending more than a minute walking the box in for Debbie and Caroline to select a truffle and then returning to the suite's living room. "And you don't have security cameras in hallways here, do you?"

He smiled at me while shaking his head. "We are a small hotel that respects our guest's privacy."

I'd thought as much. "Thank you for your help."

"Back to square one," Richard said after the manager had continued up the stairs to the second floor.

"Maybe not," I said. "We know that there wasn't much time for a stranger to see the ring box, know that the ring was worth the risk of stealing, open the box, pocket the ring, and close the box again."

"You're right. The waiter and the manager didn't spend more than a minute or two in that room. And what are the chances one of us—or Debbie or Caroline—wouldn't have noticed a stranger fiddling with something on the bed?" Richard put his hands on his hips. "Is there a chance our permanently buzzed bride forgot to put the ring in the box or took it out and forget where she hid it?"

I thought about the cocktail shaker she usually kept in her purse and the fact that her liquid diets consisted mostly of vodka cocktails. "With Debbie, there's always a chance."

CHAPTER SEVEN

"Let me get this straight." Kate glanced from me to Richard and back again as we stood outside the Jasmine suite. "You think the ring might not be stolen at all? You think Darla might have misplaced it or forgotten to pack it?"

"It's a possibility," I said, keeping my voice to a whisper. Even though there was no one else in the hallway, the hotel security chief and the general manager were just inside talking to the wedding party. "You know she can be a little ditzy when she drinks."

"Which is always," Richard added.

"But who loses a three-carat diamond ring?" Kate did not look convinced.

"Someone who has more than one?" Richard motioned with his head toward the door to the suite.

"Do we know if the ring is insured?" I asked.

"Darla says it is." Kate shifted from one high-heeled foot to the other. "I think that's the only reason Debbie and Darla aren't going into full meltdown mode. That and the champagne Fern keeps insisting they drink."

I let out a resigned breath. On a normal wedding day, Fern encouraged bubbly to calm the nerves. I could only imagine how much he was pushing to ease the loss of a diamond ring. Not that our booze-loving clients needed much of a push.

"Is the bride going to be sober enough to get down the aisle?" I asked Kate.

"You know Debbie is fully functional after drinking enough to bring down a bull elephant."

That was true. I suppose I didn't need to stress about how much she was imbibing. I probably should worry about how much Fern was drinking, though. He'd been known to get carried away and nearly process down the aisle with the bride after a few too many.

"What about the witch doctor?" I asked. "How did that go?"

Richard motioned with his hands for me to keep my voice low. "Let's not bandy out the phrase 'witch doctor.' I still don't think it would go over too well with the Episcopal priest we hired to perform the vow renewal."

"Is he here?" Kate glanced around the empty hallway. "I'd love to check that off our list."

"I haven't seen anyone who gave off a priest vibe yet," I said, lowering my voice. "So, how did the ritual go?"

Kate dragged pink polished nails through her hair. "It was my first Caribbean magic ritual, so I don't have much to judge it against, but I think it went well. Debbie and Darla loved it, especially when the priestess claimed that the ring was still nearby."

"She did?" Richard leaned closer. "Any hint as to where?"

Kate shook her head. "Nope. It was all pretty vague, but she did tell Darla that the ring was the beginning of the end."

Richard gasped. "The end? The end of what?"

"She didn't specify."

I shook my head. I was going to wring Fern's neck if this had scared my client.

Richard made a disapproving noise in the back of his throat. "Why would she say that to a bride on her wedding day? Then again, endings aren't always bad. Take the Kardashian show. I, for one, am thrilled that's ending."

"If Darla is worried about it, we're going to tell her that it means the ending of the first part of her marriage and the beginning of an entirely new and exciting chapter in their lives."

Kate grinned at me. "Nice thinking, boss."

Richard bobbed his head. "I can sell that."

"We'd better not stay out here too long." I cast my gaze toward the door. "There's currently no moderating force in there."

Richard glanced toward the stairs. "We still have so much setup to do downstairs."

Kate scooted around me. "I'll check the setup while you go get some face time with the bride."

"You sure?"

She gave me a mischievous smile. "Definitely."

"Why do I get the feeling we got the short end of that stick?" Richard said, shooting a look at Kate's retreating back.

When we walked back into the Jasmine suite, it was a different scene than before. Instead of laughter, the room buzzed with tension, and there were hushed voices from the next room. Fern still stood at the table near the French doors, but instead of working on Darla, he was now teasing her daughter Debbie's hair high over her head.

"What's going on here?" I asked through a forced smile as I appraised the halo of hair that covered the woman's face.

Fern slid his gaze to me. "I have to start out with volume in order for it to hold in this humidity."

Debbie's hand shot out and grabbed mine, even though I couldn't see her face beneath the mass of hair. "Annabelle. Have you heard?"

"Is this about the voodoo—?"

"Obeah," Fern said before I could finish my sentence.

I narrowed my gaze at him, and he hurriedly returned his attention to teasing Debbie's hair. "If you ask me, an ending is a good thing. It means out with the old and in with a new chapter in your parents' marriage."

"I hadn't thought of it like that," Debbie said, "but I meant the fact that hotel security has no leads and no idea where the ring could be. They questioned the room service waiter and the maid who came in earlier. Of course, I can't imagine any of the staff here doing such a thing. Everyone has been so lovely."

I squeezed Debbie's hand, since she couldn't see my face. "And you're sure you didn't see a thing from where you and Caroline were in the bathroom?"

"Honestly, I wasn't paying much attention." She dropped her voice. "Caroline was whining about something or other, so I was playing some music on my phone to lighten the mood and drown out her bitching. People have been in and out of here all day long."

Most getting-ready suites on weddings days were a bustle of activity with deliveries and a near constant flow of people. I was surprised more things didn't go missing from suites, especially since most brides had jewelry and rings lying around.

"Is that Annabelle?" Darla's voice came from the next room.

"Right here, Mrs. Douglas," I called back, twisting to look over to the open French doors between the rooms. Two Bahamian men, one the general manager we'd met before, and the other a beefier man I assumed was the chief of security, had their heads together in conversation near the bed while Mr. and Mrs. Douglas stood slightly apart from them. Mr. Douglas had his arm around his wife's shoulders.

I plastered on my best "everything's fine" face and approached them. "I heard there hasn't been any progress so far."

Darla nodded; her eyes wide but glassy. "Do you think we should cancel?" She clutched my hand. "We tried to cast a good omen over the day, but I don't know if it was enough."

"Don't be silly," her husband said, beating me to it. "We've been happily married for thirty years. This is just a little bump."

I was pleasantly surprised that Mr. Douglas was as cool as he was. Some dads would have been calling for heads to roll if an expensive diamond ring had disappeared. I was willing to bet that having the ring insured was a big part of his calm response.

"Your husband is absolutely right," I said.

"And as smart as he is handsome," Richard added, winking at Darla.

"Besides, you have fifty guests who've flown all this way," I reminded her. "We can't disappoint them."

"You're right. Of course, you're right." Darla fluttered a hand in front of herself. "I'm being overemotional." She giggled and hiccupped. "This doesn't make me a bridezilla, does it?"

"Of course not." Since she wasn't jumping up and down on her bouquet or insisting that all the bridesmaids go commando under their dresses so they wouldn't have panty lines, she was far from being a bridezilla. "And you look beautiful."

She blushed as her husband kissed the top of her head and said, "Just the way you looked thirty years ago."

I glanced back at Fern and noticed that Debbie's hair had not deflated much since I'd left him. "Why don't I make sure we're still on schedule while you get in your dress?"

"That's my cue to leave." Mr. Douglas gave his wife a final buss on the cheek and left the room.

"And mine to take over from Kate," Richard said, also leaving.

"Do you want me to send Debbie or Caroline in to help you?" I asked Darla, hoping she would not require my assistance with the dressing. I wasn't a prude, but I liked to avoid seeing my clients in the buff, if possible.

"Caroline went back to her room to take one of her

headache pills." Darla nudged me. "Said we were too loud for her."

That sounded like her daughter-in-law, all right. "Then I'll have Fern finish Debbie's hair and send her in."

I left Darla, told Fern to speed things up so Debbie could help her mother dress, and made a beeline for the door. I'd almost made it out when I heard a deep voice calling my name.

I turned and saw the manager walking toward me.

"You are the wedding planner? The one who made all the arrangements?"

"That's me." I held out my hand. "We didn't officially meet earlier. Annabelle Archer."

He shook my hand and inclined his head at me slightly. "Perhaps you can assist me with a delicate situation?"

"More delicate than a missing diamond ring?" I asked.

He smiled, but I could tell he was humoring me. "It's about payment."

"I submitted the client's credit card form to hold the reservation a while ago, and my assistant delivered a check when she arrived." My heart fluttered in my chest. "Didn't she?"

"She did give us a check." He frowned. "But it did not clear the bank. And when we tried to run the payment through the credit card on file, it was declined."

Now my heart was hammering, and my palms went clammy. The Douglases were ridiculously wealthy, and none of their sizable checks to wedding vendors had ever bounced. I wasn't sure what was going on, but this was very odd indeed.

CHAPTER EIGHT

"What do you mean the check bounced?" Richard's shriek reverberated off the glass walls of the dining room and caused the waiters filling water glasses to stare. "I thought it was bad enough that they'd folded the napkins into birds of paradise."

I glanced down at the white linen napkins folded to mimic the pointy, tropical flower. Richard had an aversion to any napkin fold that wasn't flat and tailored, and he was currently refolding every napkin in the room.

I motioned for him to keep it down. "I'm not sure if they heard you over on Grand Bahama Island."

He looked affronted, but lowered his voice as he unfurled a square of linen. "I don't understand. The Douglas family is loaded. We've done parties at their home. It's practically a mansion. The four-car garage is filled with one Benz after another." He dropped his voice to a near whisper. "Mr. Douglas supports his wife's taste for Birkin bags and top shelf vodka—and plenty of both."

"I know. I'm as shocked as you are, but I had the manager run everything again. There isn't enough money in the accounts to cover this event, and all the credit cards I have for them are maxed out."

Richard's perfectly arched brows rose so high I was afraid they might disappear under his choppy bangs. "But we haven't been paid yet."

"That's correct." Our flights had already been covered, but our hotel rooms were under the Douglas account. I did not relish the idea of shelling out the cash to cover the rooms for my entire team at the expensive Graycliff Hotel. "If I'd known we'd have to cover our own rooms, I would have booked us at the Comfort Inn."

Richard stopped folding a napkin and sucked in a breath. "Bite your tongue." He moved around the round table, assessing the napkins that now lay flat on top of the china dinner plates. "Being unpaid labor at an outdoor vow renewal in ninety-degree weather with one hundred percent humidity and staying at a budget hotel? I don't think so, darling."

"Let's focus on the matter at hand," I said. "What if the ring really is missing, but it was an inside job?"

"How inside?"

I glanced over my shoulder. "What if Mr. Douglas took the ring so he could get the insurance money?"

Richard moved over to the next table filled with offending napkins. "If he's broke, why buy the ring in the first place?"

"I don't know, but I'd be willing to bet that his wife knows nothing about the financial trouble. Which would explain why he couldn't just return the ring."

"I suppose so, but you'd think he would know that he couldn't cover this event." Richard threw his arms open wide. "What does he expect is going to happen when it's time to pay up? It's not like the Douglas family knows how to wash dishes." He reached out and clutched my arm in a death grip. "You don't think we're going to have to work off their bill?"

"I'm sure it won't come to that." If I knew anything about hotels, they wouldn't be serving a single plate until they had a viable payment method.

Richard pulled his phone from his pants pocket. "I'm going to check flights out tonight, just in case. If this goes south, we're flying north."

I snatched his phone from his hand. "We aren't abandoning our clients. There still might be a reasonable explanation for all this."

Richard mumbled something treasonous under his breath, but finally huffed out a breath. "So, what's your plan Miss Fix-It?"

"We should probably talk to Mr. Douglas."

Richard grimaced. "Tell the man his check bounced and his credit card is overdrawn? That sounds like a 'you' job. I'm only the general contractor you hired."

I hooked my arm through his and propelled him forward. "Yeah? Well, you're the general contractor who's going to stand next to me during an incredibly awkward conversation."

We left the dining room and passed through the lounge, where a few wedding guests were milling about around the baby grand piano.

"Honestly, darling," Richard said, as I hustled him up

the stairs. "I'm surprised you'd go for such a direct approach. You're usually much more cloak and dagger about things."

"Not about payment I'm not." I paused at the top of the stairs and peered down the carpeted hallway. "I know his room is down this way somewhere." I did remember watching him walk away from the Jasmine suite earlier. I focused hard, envisioning him walking down the hallway and pausing in front of a hotel room door. "I think this is it."

Richard pointed to the crack in the door. It wasn't closed all the way. My pulse fluttered. Open doors were never a good sign in a crime investigation.

"Should we knock?" I whispered.

My best friend gave me a scandalized look. "Of course, we should knock." He raised his own hand and rapped sharply on the door. "Mr. Douglas. It's Annabelle Archer and Richard Gerard."

The door opened even farther, but there was no reply from inside.

"I hear something," I said. It was muffled, but there were definite noises coming from inside. I pushed the door open even more, getting a view of an empty hotel room.

Richard grasped my arm. "We can't go inside."

"I hear something. Mr. Douglas might be in trouble." I stepped inside, peering around the room. Like the rest of the hotel, the bedroom featured tropical shades of peach and green with floral-printed fabrics hanging from the windows. The king-sized bed had four posters, and a ceiling fan swirled lazily over it. The bed was neatly made with a suit laid out across the duvet.

Richard followed behind me. "We aren't even sure this is the right room. If a stranger walks in on us, darling, I am not waiting for you. I'm running."

"That's the suit the men in bridal party are wearing for the ceremony." I waved a hand toward the bed. "This is his room."

Once I was inside, I could determine that the muffled sounds were coming from the attached bathroom. I put a finger to my lips and walked closer.

The bathroom door was also cracked, with steam coming from the opening. Had Mr. Douglas been taking a shower? Was that why he didn't respond to Richard's knock. Suddenly, the prospect of being in the dad's room when he walked from the bathroom seemed like a bad idea. I froze and turned on my heel.

"Let's get out of here," I mouthed to Richard.

"You don't have to tell me twice." Richard backed away from the bathroom, still facing me.

"I'm telling you, Hank," a deep male voice boomed from inside the bathroom. "I need that money transferred today."

Richard and I both stopped moving, and his mouth fell open. We were in the right room, all right. That was Mr. Douglas, and he did not sound happy.

"What do you mean there isn't enough?" Mr. Douglas shouted. "That account should have twice as much as I need to move."

Richard motioned for us to continue leaving, but I held

up a finger. I wanted to hear what was going on. This was obviously connected to the bounced check.

"I can't get into this now, Hank, but I don't know what you're talking about. I haven't been shifting money to outside accounts." He paused. "What do you mean Carlton did it? He has no reason to be touching that account."

The water in the sink was turned on and then off again, and Mr. Douglas groaned. "I can't deal with this now. Just transfer the funds from any account. I don't care what you have to do, but that money needs to be in my account within the hour. My wife can never know about any of this."

There was the beep of a call being disconnected and footsteps padding toward us.

Richard slapped a hand over his mouth. There was no time for us to make it across the room and out the door. I motioned to the bed and dove for the floor. Richard hit the floor on the other side, both of us rolling underneath and out of sight as the bathroom door swung open.

I held my breath and twisted my head to see Richard's shadowed face glaring at me as we both lay underneath the bed, the only light coming from the inch or so between the dust ruffle and the floor. He blew a dust bunny away from his face, his eyes narrowing into slits.

I'd seen my best friend outraged plenty of times, but this was next level indignation.

Then my phone began to vibrate in my pocket.

CHAPTER NINE

"That was too close," I whispered, hurrying down the hall-way, away from the room.

"Who do we have to thank for almost getting caught cowering under a bed?" Richard asked, his face both flushed and dusty.

I glanced down at the missed call on my screen. "Reese."

Luckily, I'd been able to disconnect the call before it had continued buzzing, and Mr. Douglas had been too busy muttering darkly to himself to notice. Still, I was pretty sure I'd lost a year off my life.

"I'm assuming you won't be telling your cop husband why you couldn't answer his call?"

"You assume correctly."

Richard mumbled something about hiding more of my secrets as he flicked dust off his hair, and we bustled down the stairs. "If it didn't involve an awkward explana-tion, I would read the housekeeping staff the riot act. The dust bunnies under that bed were so plentiful I was afraid they were going to start forming herds and attacking."

"We don't have time for you to read anyone the riot act." I stopped at the bottom of the stairs and brushed the front of my dress, which carried streaks of dust. "We just lost thirty minutes listening to Mr. Douglas dress."

Richard wrinkled his nose. "I feel so tawdry."

"It's not like we watched."

"At least we didn't get caught." Richard dropped his voice as we walked through the lobby and the parlor with the grand piano.

Several well-dressed guests sat clustered on couches, and I assumed they were early for the wedding. I smiled and tried to act natural, even though I was having an internal panic attack. We were no closer to finding the missing diamond ring, but we were closing in on go-time for the wedding.

"At least we know why the check bounced," I said, matching Richard's low tone as we entered the dining room.

"But it sounds like Mr. Douglas was as surprised as anyone."

I sighed. "Which means that he probably didn't steal his own wife's ring for the insurance money. If he didn't know he was short on funds, that eliminates his motive."

"So, we're back to square one." Richard put his hands on his hips as he surveyed the tables set for the reception. "And I'm back to refolding napkins."

I swiped a loose strand of hair off my forehead. "But what are the chances that the ring goes missing and there's a financial issue with the Douglases all at the same time? It seems like a pretty crazy coincidence to me."

Richard picked up an elaborately folded napkin and unfurled it into the air. "Maybe, but from what we heard, Mr. Douglas isn't the one involved with moving money from his accounts."

"That's right. It was Carlton, and that surprised him."

Richard refolded the white square of linen into a perfect rectangle with knife-sharp creases. "What if Carlton is the one who's behind all of this?"

I grasped the back of one of the mahogany chairs. What did I know about the Douglas son, aside from the fact that he worked for his father's company and was married to the most uptight human I'd ever met?

Carlton had always seemed pleasant enough, but I'd never spent much time with him. Even when we'd planned his wedding to Caroline, his mother and sister had done most of the legwork until the bride arrived. And then Caroline had promptly undone nearly all of it. But aside from his questionable taste in wives, the guy Kate referred to as Prep School Ken had always been perfectly nice to us. Could I see him as a thief and an embezzler? And would he really steal from his own family? Talk about biting the hand that feeds you.

Richard handed me a napkin. "If you're going to stand there looking gob smacked, at least you can fold."

I took the napkin and instinctively creased it into a flat fold design. I'd folded enough napkins that I could do it in my sleep. "So how do we find out if Carlton is the one behind all this?"

Richard gave me an arch look. "We could always sneak

into his room and crawl under his bed while he dresses. Or hide behind his curtains. Aren't those your usual techniques for investigating?"

Mack's step faltered as he approached us, his wide grin morphing into surprise. "Do I want to know?"

"I've only had to do that twice, okay, maybe three times." I shot Richard a look and turned to Mack. "It's not as bad as it sounds."

He didn't look convinced, but he shrugged. "We finished all the outside decor, although we'll need to keep spritzing the blooms, so they don't wilt."

I scanned the long room. "Is that what Buster's doing?"

Mack nodded. "He's down at the ceremony site so he can freshen up the arrangements after photos."

Photos! I pulled out my phone, glancing at it quickly. The day was flying by, and I'd barely checked anything off my wedding day schedule. I'd gotten so distracted by the missing ring and bounced check that I didn't even know where we were in the process.

"Is it already time for pre-wedding photos?" Richard gasped, swiveling his head to take in the dining room. Half the tables had napkins folded like birds-of-paradise and half had his refolded napkins lying flat on the plates. "That means we don't have long before guests will be coming through here on the way to the ceremony. Fold faster, Annabelle!"

"I really should check on Kate and the bridal party," I said as he thrust another napkin at me.

"Are you going to abandon me here after you dragged me under the groom's bed for half an hour?"

Mack's pierced eyebrow shot heavenward. "Sometimes I'm so glad my work is behind the scenes."

Before I could assure Mack that Richard was teasing, and it wasn't as inappropriate as it sounded, my phone rang again. I glanced at the screen. It was my husband. Again.

Richard cut his eyes to my phone. "You'd better answer the poor man before he sends the cavalry out looking for you."

I answered, as I walked a few steps away from Richard and Mack. "Hey, sorry I couldn't pick up earlier. It's been crazy."

Mike exhaled loudly on the other end. "I just wanted to make sure you arrived safely and hadn't killed Richard yet."

I laughed, but it felt forced. "No murder yet."

"Babe? Why do you sound weird?" His voice dropped an octave. "Are you sure there hasn't been a murder?"

"There isn't a death at every wedding I plan." I attempted to sound indignant.

He was silent.

"Fine," I huffed out a breath. "There has been a theft."

"What kind of theft?" He'd assumed his detective voice.

"The bride's ring went missing while she was getting ready. I was in the suite when it disappeared but there were so many people in and out—and no one near it for the time it would take to open the ring box and snatch the ring out—that it's impossible to pinpoint who could have taken it or how."

"I'm assuming it's an expensive ring?"

"Two carat platinum and diamond."

He let out a low whistle. "And it was sitting out?"

"It was on the bed with the veil and other bridal accessories so the photographer could take some pictures. But it was in the closed ring box. And only the ring was taken, not the box."

"That's odd," my husband said. "Why not just snatch the box?"

I hadn't really thought about that, but he was right. It would have been easier to take the box entirely than to open it, take out the ring, and close the box, leaving it on the bed. "Maybe so that no one would notice it gone at first."

"And they didn't have any place to hide the bulk of the ring box," he said.

I thought back to everyone who'd come in and out of the room. That narrowed the field. The room service waiter and manager could have hidden a ring box in their uniform jackets, but there was one person who couldn't hide a thing in his tight leather pants.

Mack.

CHAPTER TEN

"Reese thinks Mack did it?" Richard gaped at me after I'd hung up and rejoined him in folding napkins. Luckily, Mack had left to put the finishing touches on the escort card arrangement on the baby grand piano, so he didn't hear Richard's near shriek.

I shushed my best friend, glancing over my shoulder. "Of course, he doesn't. He was merely making a point about why someone would pocket the ring without the box."

Richard tapped a finger on his chin. "He does have a point."

My husband had also made the point that I should call in the local police to deal with the theft instead of relying on hotel security, a move I wholeheartedly agreed with but one that wasn't my call. It did make me wonder why Mr. Douglas hadn't insisted on the police being called.

"You don't think that Mr. Douglas not wanting to get the authorities involved means he took the ring—or suspects he knows who took it?" I asked, smoothing a napkin out on the table.

Richard tapped his finger faster. "You mean, does he suspect his own son? That would explain why he's not more upset and insisting the hotel be searched from top to bottom."

The knot that had been forming in my stomach since Reese had talked through the case with me now tightened. "It would explain a lot, including how calm he's been about the theft. If he suspects his son and knows he'll get the insurance payout anyway, he wouldn't have any reason to get worked up."

Richard made a harumping sound and unfurled another napkin before he began to refold it. "Which means we shouldn't spend any more time worrying about it. If the man who bought the ring doesn't want the thief caught, then we shouldn't be falling all over ourselves to solve the crime."

He had a point, but I hated to give up so easily. My instinct to fix every wedding problem made the idea of giving up almost unbearable. Before I could argue why we should keep looking, an armful of flowers appeared in one of the doorways leading into the main hotel. The long, bare legs and high heel mules underneath left me in no doubt as to who was carrying the bouquets.

"Annabelle?" Kate asked from behind the tropical flowers.

"Is everyone ready for photos?" I asked, handing Richard back his napkins and ignoring his spluttered protests as I walked over to her.

She poked her head about the flowers. "Fern is right behind me with the bridal party."

I peered over her shoulder and saw a flash of the hairdresser's brightly colored top as he held Darla's arm and bustled her toward the back door leading to the pool.

"Coming through!" Fern called, waving away a nonexistent crowd.

The bride wore a simple ivory organza gown that draped in the front, and Debbie and Caroline followed in mango-colored chiffon sundresses. Behind them were several men in perfectly tailored blue suits with white open-necked shirts, all of them looking like they'd stepped out of a Ralph Lauren catalogue. I recognized Mr. Douglas, his son Carlton, and Debbie's husband. I gave a mental sigh of relief that Kate had already pinned on all the boutonnières. One less thing to do, and one more thing I could check off my list.

"I'll come down with you to help get it all started," I told Kate, then pivoted back to Richard. "Then I'll come back up and figure out our next steps."

"If I don't hear from you, I'll start knotting these napkins so we can escape out the windows," Richard said in a stage whisper.

"What's he talking about?" Kate asked, as we walked through the hotel, out the French doors to the back garden, and started down the stone steps.

I considered telling Kate that we might not get paid, but decided that the fewer people that knew, the better. Besides, I felt obliged to make the day nice for Darla, and I wanted everyone on board with that plan. After all, it wasn't her fault that her son might be embezzling her husband's money, and she'd always been a wonderful client.

Sweat trailed down my back as we walked the last few steps onto the pool deck. The rectangular pool stretched out long, an ornate swirling pattern of blue tiles on the pool floor catching my eye. String lights were already draped high above the water for later that evening, and high tables covered in white cloths dotted the stone pool deck. Tall trees and lush palms shaded the area, casting shadows across the water.

The photographer had the bridal party positioned in front of some pink bougainvillea at the far end, so Kate and I hurried to join them and distribute the flowers. Kate handed the bride and bridesmaids their bouquets while I paused in front of Mr. Douglas.

I knew I should say something, but I wasn't sure how to tell the man that his check had bounced, and his credit card was maxed out. Before I could find the words, he turned to me.

"I don't suppose the hotel security staff has made any headway in finding my wife's ring?"

"Not that I've heard." Another reason I doubted he'd taken the ring himself. Why bother asking if he knew where it was. Then again, if he'd been the one to take it, it was also a good way to cover his tracks. "At least it was insured."

His cheeks flushed and his eyes dropped. "Actually, I hadn't gotten around to insuring it yet." He cleared his throat. "There's been a lot going on lately."

Was he serious? From the way he clenched his jaw, I

suspected he was telling the truth. "So, you won't be getting an insurance payout?"

He seemed a little surprised by my blunt question, but he shook his head. "No, which is why I'm hoping the hotel comes through for me."

So much for my theory that Mr. Douglas was willing to let the thief get away with stealing the ring because he'd get the insurance money.

"Now I need all the family," the photographer called out, and Mr. Douglas dutifully left me to stand by his wife.

As I watched the Douglas family pose and smile, my gaze went to the Douglas son. Mr. Douglas also glanced at Carlton a few too many times as the photographer arranged them in a neat row with their bodies angled in toward the bride. The furtive looks made me think Mr. Douglas hadn't yet approached his son about the missing money. Apparently, he hated awkward money conversations on wedding days as well.

My stomach clenched into a hard knot as I thought about what I now knew. The ring wasn't insured, the family couldn't pay for the party, and I had zero suspects with both motive and opportunity.

CHAPTER ELEVEN

"Can I ask why you look like you're about to swoon, sweetie?" Fern sidled up to me as the family photos continued.

I'd been lost in my own thoughts—thoughts which included us being run out on a rail from the hotel—and hadn't realized I'd braced my hand on the edge of a nearby table so hard my fingers were turning white. I jerked my head up to see Fern's worried face and released my grip on the table. "Nothing. I'm fine. Just thinking about the schedule."

Fern pursed his lips, then shook his head. "You never look that way when you're thinking about wedding day timing. Your 'schedule face' is much more animated. This resembles your 'the limos went to the wrong hotel' face. Or your "the ring bearer wet his pants' face."

I almost groaned. This was the problem with working with a team who knew you so well. They knew you too well, and it was hard to pull one over on them. "Fine. I'm worried about the missing ring."

"Now that I believe." Fern stood next to me; his body angled toward the clients while we watched the photo session. "Too bad the priestess didn't give us much in the way of leads, although at least we know the ring is still close by."

If we believe the priestess, I thought. "I suppose it does make more sense that it would be an inside job. It always seemed a bit of a stretch that someone from the hotel would know about the ring and be able to pocket it so quickly without being noticed."

Fern nodded. "Not to mention the staff has been lovely. I can't imagine any of them stealing."

"You only say that because they've been refilling the champagne buckets all day."

He gave me an arch smile. "Good service is good service, sweetie."

I turned my attention back to the family photos, studying Mr. Douglas as he stood next to his wife with a wide smile on his face. My theory that he'd stolen the ring to get the insurance payout was now a bust for more than one reason. Not only was there no insurance for the ring, it appeared that the man only learned that his accounts were empty after the ring disappeared.

I shifted my gaze to his son, Carlton. From what I'd overheard while huddled under the bed with Richard, the money has been transferred from the Douglas business accounts by Carlton without his father's knowledge. That moved him right to the top of the suspect list except for one small issue. He hadn't been in the bridal suite when the ring vanished. Was it possible the missing ring and the missing money were two separate, yet highly coincidental, issues?

I sighed, thinking about my husband, DC police detective Mike Reese's thoughts about coincidences in investigations. He didn't believe in them.

"Far be it from me to judge," Fern said as he eyed me and then the family portrait session in progress. "But are you checking out Debbie's brother?"

I tore my gaze from Carlton, my cheeks warming. "Of course not."

"I would hope not. You're still a newlywed and you've got a hunky husband waiting for you at home." Fern waggled his eyebrows. "And he carries handcuffs."

I swatted at Fern. "Not at home, he doesn't."

Fern frowned. "Pity."

"I was only looking at Carlton because of something Richard and I discovered." I lowered my voice, deciding to throw caution to the wind and confide in Fern, since he usually had a good take on people. "He's been embezzling from his father's company, and I'm trying to decide if that makes him a more likely suspect regarding the missing ring."

Fern's eyes grew wide. "Embezzlement?" He darted a glance at the family, positioned perfectly in front of the cascading fuchsia bougainvillea. "But he looks so…"

I glanced at Carlton's stiffly coifed, hair. "Upstanding?"

"I was going to say boring. It's hard to imagine anyone with that haircut doing something as daring as embezzling."

I was about to tell him that you couldn't judge a

person's proclivity to crime by a haircut when I stopped myself. Maybe you could. Fern had been right about people in the past based on hairstyle, and he lived and died by the belief that you should never trust anyone with micro bangs or a mullet. Carlton sported a seriously uptight haircut that hadn't changed in all the years I'd known the Douglas family. It matched his very preppy, and according to Fern, boring persona. Could I imagine Carlton being daring enough to steal from his own family?

"Even if he embezzled the money, he wasn't anywhere near the ring when it went missing," I said, shaking my head.

"Or so we think. Nondescript people can slip in and out of places without anyone noticing them." He smoothed the front of his brightly colored tunic. "It's why I could never join the CIA. I'm too unforgettable."

"Yes, that's the reason," I deadpanned.

He shot me a withering look before straightening and touching a hand to his ponytail. "If you want to know if he has the ring, there are ways of finding out."

Before I could ask what ways he meant, Fern rushed over to the family with his hands in the air. "Wait! Stop everything!"

I sucked in a breath and gripping the edge of the table again. What was he doing?

"These jackets need to be straightened," he said as he bustled behind the wedding party and began tugging their jackets and flattening his hands across them as if he was frisking for weapons.

The photographer lowered her camera and watched

open-mouthed as Fern manhandled all the groomsmen so quickly that they didn't have time to protest. Then he rushed back and stood in front of them. "Much better. Carry on!"

He walked back to me, muttering from the side of his mouth without turning around, "No rings in pockets."

"Thanks," I said as all the men exchanged confused glances, but returned to posing for the photographer. "But I didn't think Carlton would bring the ring with him to the wedding."

Fern's face fell. "Good point. He must have stashed it someplace in the hotel for safekeeping until everything cools down." He peered up at the historic hotel. "Where did the smugglers hide things in the past?"

"I have a feeling the pirates and smugglers who used this place had booty that was bigger than a single ring."

Fern released a dramatic sigh. "So, it could be anywhere."

"Pretty much." I joined him in sighing. The odds of us finding the ring in time for the quickly approaching wedding were starting to look slim.

He held his palms up. "I can assure you that it isn't in the ladies' hair. There's no place to hide the ring in those bobs despite all the volume I gave them." He wrinkled his nose. "And Caroline's hair is so straight it can't even hold a wave."

I would have found his comments bizarre if we hadn't once nabbed a thief who'd stashed diamonds in overly bouffant wedding hair.

Fern perked up. "Have we checked the bouquets yet?"

I put a hand on his arm. I did not want him going at

the bouquets with the same gusto he'd used to investigate the men's pockets. "Buster and Mack will have your head if you ruin their bouquets."

Fern cut his gaze to Buster standing nearby with a spray bottle, his thick, tattooed arms folded over his barrel chest. "Perhaps it can wait." He patted my arm. "Look at it this way, sweetie. At least no one's died."

Kate joined us, her arms no longer filled with bouquets, but now holding the women's clutch purses. "Yet."

CHAPTER TWELVE

"What do you mean?" Fern's gaze darted around the dense foliage surrounding the pool. "Do you think we're in danger? You don't think the hotel still attracts a criminal crowd, do you?"

"Because it was built by a pirate and popular with gangsters?" I asked.

Kate shifted the purses in her arms. "Nothing like that. I just mean Caroline might kill someone if she has to stand outside much longer."

We all glanced at the sister-in-law who stood stiffly at the end of the family row, her lips tight. Since Kate and I had planned Caroline's wedding to Carlton, we knew all about her prickly personality.

"What's wrong with her now?" Fern said with a sigh. He'd never gotten over the blonde insisting on wearing her hair stick-straight for her wedding, giving him nothing to do but attach a veil. A task he bitterly claimed that a trained monkey could have done.

"Allergies, heat rash, who knows?" Kate shrugged. "Her finger is breaking out. Remember how it did at her wedding, Annabelle?"

I did remember. It turned out that Caroline was one of the very few people in the world who was allergic to platinum and had broken out in localized hives around her ring finger during the wedding rehearsal. She was so hysterical about it, she'd insisted on wearing gloves during the ceremony and her husband had been forced to shove it onto her gloved finger, where it had promptly gotten stuck. The couple had been late to their own reception while we'd attempted to get it off.

"How could she possibly have a reaction now?" I asked. "She doesn't wear her platinum ring anymore."

Carlton had gotten her an equally impressive 24-carat gold version of her wedding ring, which she wore instead.

"Beats me." Kate wrinkled her nose. "Maybe it's a rash from the heat."

"It is warm out here." Fen scratched at his arms. "I hope I don't get a rash."

I wagged a finger at both of them. "Don't even think about it. No one is allowed to get heat rash or heat stroke. I have enough to deal with, thank you very much."

Fern muttered something but my eyes were trained on Caroline as she nervously scratched at her finger.

I spun around to face Fern. "Can you handle this? Kate and I need to check on something in the hotel." I grasped his arm. "And can you make sure they don't come back up to the hotel until we get back? It's crucial."

"Keep them down here?" He cut his gaze to the photographer, who appeared to be wrapping up.

"Yes. Make sure they don't come back up to the hotel for any reason until we come back out. Create a distraction if you have to."

Fern's pupils widened. "Is this about the missing ring?"

"I hope so," I told him.

He gave me a determined look and a brusque nod. "You know I'm excellent at distractions, sweetie." Fern fluttered a hand at me. "You two run on. I'll keep them busy down here."

Despite a pang of nervousness at what kind of distraction Fern would think up, I grabbed Kate by the elbow and walked quickly toward the stairs.

"Where are we going?" she asked, craning her head to look behind her. "Shouldn't I leave the purses?"

"Nope." I hurried her up the stone steps and into the hotel. We passed Richard, still refolding napkins in the dining room, but didn't stop.

He poked his head out of the doorway. "Why are you two in such a hurry?"

"We're off to find a diamond ring," I said.

He tossed the napkin he was working on to the table. "You know where it is?"

"We're about to find out if my hunch is right," I said, as he fell in step behind us walking up the stairs.

When we reached the top of the landing, I motioned to the purses. "Which one is Caroline's?"

Kate stared at me. "Caroline's? The sister-in-law?"

I took one of the silver purses and snapped it open. "Is it this one?"

Kate pushed another purse at me. "It's this one." She

nibbled the corner of her lip. "Annabelle, are you sure about this?"

"No. That's why we need to search her room."

Richard held his hands up, palms out. "Hold on a minute. No one said anything about searching rooms. I've had enough of unauthorized room visits, thank you very much."

"No one asked you to come," I told him, locating the room key in the purse and holding it up. "If I'm right, we can find the ring and return it to the Douglases."

Richard's eyes were unblinking. "And if you're wrong?"

"We make a mad dash for the airport."

"Why do I always hate your plans?" Richard muttered. "I'm still getting dust out of my hair from the last one."

"That was less of a plan and more of a last resort so we didn't get caught."

"It's fine," Kate said. "They're still doing photos."

"And Fern promised to keep them distracted," I added, as I walked down the hallway until I reached the proper room.

"I'm only doing this because I know there's nothing more distracting than Fern," Richard hissed as he trailed behind me.

The hallway was deserted as we clustered around the door. I opened it with the key, pushing the wooden door and waving everyone inside. This guest room was smaller than the others we'd been in, but the decor was just as floral and fussy. Pink and green chintz curtains hung from the high windows, and white palm trees were painted in stucco on the walls.

"Fan out," I whispered, closing the door behind us. "If I'm right, Caroline hid the ring somewhere in her room."

"Is this because of the finger rash?" Kate asked, crossing to the bed and opening the drawers of the dark wood nightstand.

I walked to the vanity with a pale-pink upholstered stool tucked up underneath. "I think she must have put the ring on her finger, probably with the diamonds facing her palm, and left the suite like that. After the ring disappeared, she came back to her room, right?"

"That's right," Kate said, peeking under the striped throw pillows on the bed. "And it didn't occur to me to look at her hands for a ring."

"Who would?" I said, moving the objects on the vanity, then glancing over to where Richard was standing in front of the door. "Are you going to help us?"

He folded his arms over his chest. "I cannot believe you're searching a client's room."

"Technically, she's not our client," Kate said.

Richard tapped one foot rapidly on the hardwood floor. "She's a former bride."

"But the Douglases paid for that wedding, too," I reminded him. "They've been our best clients ever. I don't care if they're going through tough times right now. I can't let their own daughter-in-law steal from them."

"I thought Carlton was the one embezzling the money," Richard said.

"Embezzling?" Kate jerked up. "When did this become about embezzling?"

I'd forgotten that Kate didn't know about the bounced check, the maxed-out credit card, and the empty Douglas

JEWEL OF THE AISLE: A NOVELLA

bank accounts. "It's a bit of a long story, but someone has been moving money from the Douglas company accounts."

"Carlton," Richard whispered.

Kate's jaw dropped. "He's stealing from his own father's company? But why? I thought he got a baller salary."

I shrugged. "I haven't figured it all out yet, but I'm guessing Carlton and Caroline were in this together. It has to be connected."

"Like Bonnie and Clyde," Richard said, his voice a mixture of shock and awe.

"That's awful." Kate pursed her lips. "Debbie and Darla Douglas might be lushes, but they're great tippers, and they never treat us like the help."

"And Mr. Douglas has always paid everything way in advance—including our tips," I said. "They don't deserve to be robbed by their own family."

Richard huffed out a breath. "When you put it like that, I suppose I have to help."

Before he could join us, the door flew open. As the door hit his back, Richard pitched forward, landing face first on the floor with a scream. Caroline stood in the doorway; her face wild as she scratched viscously at her finger. She was soaking wet, and her pale hair was matted to her face. Fern stood next to her, also dripping water.

I had so many questions, I didn't know where to begin.

"What are you doing in my room?" she screamed.

The room was silent, except for Kate, who drew her hand out from under the mattress and held up a sparkling diamond ring. "Found it!"

Caroline snarled, shooting murderous glances at all of us before turning on her heel and running down the hall.

I pulled Richard up—leaving him squawking in place and dusting off his clothes—and then ran out into the hall. Just in time to see Carlton Douglas—Caroline's husband —holding his wife firmly by the arm.

"Not so fast, honey," he said. "I have a few questions for you first."

CHAPTER THIRTEEN

I stared at Carlton as the rest of his family rushed up the stairs behind him. Luckily, Caroline was the only one who was dripping wet, although everyone else looked thoroughly confused.

"Let go of me!" Caroline jerked her arm, but her husband held tight.

Kate emerged from Caroline and Carlton's room, holding the ring between her fingers. "Is anyone looking for this?"

Darla put her hands to her cheeks and gasped. "You found it!"

"This is why you're the best wedding planners in the world," Debbie said. "Even with all the dead bodies."

I tried not to blanch at this backhanded compliment and fought to urge to remind her that there had still been no murders at any of the events we'd planned for them.

Carlton's usually placid face was contorted with anger

as he stared at the ring and then at his wife. "It was hidden in our room?"

Caroline pressed her lips together in an even thinner line than usual, refusing to answer even as she shot daggers at my assistant.

"Under the mattress," Kate said, walking it over to Darla, who promptly slid it onto her finger with a sigh.

"I don't know how to thank you enough." Mr. Douglas stepped forward, patting Kate on the shoulder.

"It was all of us," Kate said, glancing back to me, a soaking Fern, and Richard rubbing his chin from where he'd landed on the floor face first.

Finally, Caroline spoke, her blazing eyes settling on me. "How did you know?"

I flicked my gaze to her fingers, which she scratched absently. "The allergic reaction to the platinum."

She cursed colorfully enough to make Kate's eyebrows lift and me to be glad that our Christian biker florists hadn't heard it. "I saw you and Kate run off during photos and I thought you might have figured it out. I tried to follow you, but…" Her gaze drifted to Fern, who was squeezing water from his ponytail onto the carpet.

He shrugged. "You said to keep everyone away from the hotel and to create a distraction."

"How did you know?" I asked Carlton. "I thought you were…"

"Involved?" Carlton laughed bitterly. "Before my wife took an untimely dip in the pool, my father pulled me aside and confronted me about the missing money."

"Missing money?" Darla looked from her husband to her son. "What missing money?"

No one spoke for a moment, so I cleared my throat. "The check for the wedding didn't clear, and the credit card on file was maxed out. That's when we figured out that there was something going on that was bigger than just a stolen ring."

Darla's eyes were saucers as she stared at her husband. "How could the check not clear? That account has plenty of funds in it."

"Not as of today it didn't," Mr. Douglas admitted. "My manager confirmed that the funds had all been transferred using Carlton's codes."

Everyone's eyes swung to the son, who vigorously shook his head. "It wasn't me. I would never do something like that to my own family, my own company."

Mr. Douglas put a hand on his son's shoulder. "I'm sorry I suspected you."

Carlton shook his head. "I don't blame you. The evidence pointed to me. We were all fooled." He slid his gaze to his wife, who glared at him defiantly. "Even when I got a call from one of my credit cards about being maxed out, I didn't want to believe it. Only when I discovered that my personal access code had been used to transfer company funds did I know Caroline was behind it."

"She knew your codes?" His sister asked, shooting a death glare at her sister-in-law.

Carlton's cheeks colored. "I write them down along with all my passwords, so I won't forget them. She knows where I keep that list."

"Why?" Darla stepped forward, her attention focused on Caroline. "We treated you like a daughter."

Caroline's defiant expression faltered for a moment,

then hardened. "I never wanted to be a daughter. I wanted to be a success. I wanted to be somebody." She spit out the last few words.

Carlton blinked at her. "But you are successful. Your corporate gifting business has been getting tons of publicity."

"Because I've been paying for it," Caroline snapped. "The business has been in the red for over a year now."

Her husband opened and closed his mouth like a fish searching for water. "A year? You never said anything."

"You have no idea what it's like. You come from money, and you stepped into a successful business. I had none of that. Everything I've gotten has been on my own, and it's been a struggle." Her voice wavered before regaining its steely edge. "I couldn't bear to admit that I'd failed."

Kate exchanged a glance with me that told me she felt at least a twinge of sympathy for the woman, despite how difficult she was and despite her crimes.

"So instead of telling me you needed help, you stole from me and my family?" Carlton's voice ached with hurt, and I felt like an intruder even standing in the hallway.

"I planned to pay it all back," Caroline said. "I only thought I'd need a little to cover expenses, and I'd been able to return it before anyone noticed."

"But you didn't," he said.

"I couldn't. I needed more, and by then it was easy to siphon it off and forget that it wasn't mine."

Her husband raked a hand through his perfectly side swept hair. "And the ring?"

She dropped her gaze to the floor. "It was too good to

be true when I saw the ring box sitting out on the bed. I assumed it was insured so your father wouldn't be out the money, but if I sold it, I could have paid back everything and even had some left over to try to save my business." She let out a weary sigh. "I waited until there was a lot of commotion and slipped the ring onto my finger then made an excuse to run back to our room and get my customized foundation."

There was uneasy shifting as we all stood in the hall-way, Caroline and Fern still dripping pool water onto the carpet.

"Was it always about the money?" Carlton asked.

Caroline bit the edge of her lip but wouldn't meet his eyes. Before she could respond, the hotel manager and security chief came up the stairs with a Bahamian police officer in a long white jacket over dark pants, his hat tucked under his arm.

"I understand the ring was located, and the culprit discovered," the hotel manager said, his gaze falling on Caroline, who was still being held by Carlton.

There was another heavy silence, but then Caroline cleared her throat. "It was me. I took the ring."

"And does the owner of the ring wish to press charges?" the police officer asked.

Mr. Douglas opened his mouth while he shook his head, but Caroline preempted anything he had to say. "I'm ready to be charged."

Darla and Debbie both gasped, but Carlton released her arm as the police officer stepped forward. Darla clutched her husband by the hand and shook her head as Caroline was led down the stairs and from the hotel.

"Why does this not feel as triumphant as I thought it would?" Kate whispered to me.

I agreed. Even though I'd found Caroline to be a royal pain in the backside, watching Carlton discover his wife's duplicity had not been pleasant to watch.

"Carlton," his mother said, reaching out a hand. "I'm so sorry."

Carlton gave his head a brusque shake. "I'm the one who should be apologizing. If I'd been paying better attention, my wife wouldn't have been able to siphon so much money from our company."

Mr. Douglas put an arm around his shoulders. "It's nothing that can't be fixed. Besides, the company has reserve accounts that even you can't access. My manager has already shifted funds."

Richard released a breath. "Oh, thank heavens."

I glanced around at the family. "I know this is awkward, but what do you want to do about the vow renewal?"

"We're doing it," Carlton said before anyone else could speak. "We're still here to celebrate my parents, and that's what we're going to do."

"Are you sure?" Debbie asked.

He nodded. "I need something to take my mind off what happened. Tomorrow I'll go down and talk to Caroline, but for now, we have a happy marriage to celebrate."

"And we'll even be on time to start," Richard said.

Kate grinned. "The miracles never crease."

"Cease," Richard and I both said in unison under our breath.

CHAPTER FOURTEEN

"So, let me see if I understand this correctly," Buster said as we sat around the pool later than evening. "The daughter-in-law was behind all of it?"

The guests were in the middle of dinner in the dining room, so we'd snuck off for a little down time before the wedding moved to the pool deck for after-dinner drinks and dancing. The string lights crisscrossed over the pool were on, making the water below twinkle. The band was set up at the far side of the long pool, but the band members had yet to take their places, and the bar was fully outfitted, although the bartenders weren't on duty.

"All of it," I said. We'd tried to bring Buster and Mack up to speed, but things had quickly devolved into a hustle to get the ceremony started and the bride down the aisle.

"Annabelle was right about her snatching the ring," Kate said, kicking off her heels and stretching her legs out in front of her. "We just didn't know why or that it was connected to the dad's bounced check."

Mack stroked a hand down his goatee. "Who knew it was all so connected?"

"At first I thought Carlton had been behind it or they were working together," I said. "I hadn't imagined that Caroline had gotten his passcodes."

"Well, if you write them all down…" Richard said, his words trailing off.

"Even I know not to do that," Kate muttered.

"How did she plan to get away with it?" Buster rubbed his bald head. "The family would find out, eventually."

"And apparently, Carlton had already gotten suspicious," I said.

Richard brushed some invisible lint from his suit, which he'd been doing since he fell. "That's why he stopped her when she ran. He'd gotten a call about unusual activity on one of his cards earlier and finally realized his wife was behind it. "

"At least he had enough on his other cards to cover all of this," Mack said.

The Douglas's son had been more than happy to step in and cover the event, probably because he was so embarrassed that his wife had almost ruined his family. Of course, she'd been hauled off to a Bahamian jail. The vow renewal ceremony had gone off without a hitch—at least without another one—and no one had seemed too broken up about it.

"Apparently, Mr. Douglas thinks he can get a lot of it back," I said. "Caroline had a decent amount of it still sitting in her personal account, no doubt to set her up in her new life."

Kate leaned forward and dropped her voice. "She had a second plane ticket leaving tonight."

"Cheese and crackers!" Mack sucked in a sharp breath. "She was planning on running off?"

Kate nodded, clearly relishing every bit of the story we'd gotten from the hotel manager after Caroline had been taken away. "That two-bit hussy was going to leave her husband, take the ring, and disappear."

"I couldn't have said it better myself," Fern said as he stepped behind the bar. He'd changed from his soaking wet Junkanoo tunic and was in a white linen jacket with a fuchsia flower pinned to his lapel. "What's everyone drinking?" He grabbed a pitcher of red punch. "Actually, what am I saying? I'm not a bartender. Everyone's having punch!"

"Punch sounds perfect—as long as it's spiked." Richard flopped into a wrought iron pool chair. "This day has been too much."

"Would I ever serve you punch that wasn't spiked?" Fern asked with a laugh.

"Back to Caroline for a moment." Mack rubbed his head as if he was confused. "She was really going to run off?"

"When they got her to the police station and started digging, they discovered she'd changed her reservations to a plane leaving tonight."

"And to think I felt sorry for her," Kate said. "Especially when she was going on about not growing up rich like the Douglas family and wanting to save her business."

"Then we find out that she'd been willing to ditch her husband to save her skin," I added.

"Did she really think she'd be able to vanish?" Buster asked.

"She always struck me as a bit delusional," Richard said. "She did have a December wedding with cacti instead of florals."

Mack groaned. "Don't remind me."

I twisted to where Fern was pouring glasses of punch. "I still don't understand why you and Caroline were soaking wet."

"Let's just say my distraction got a little out of hand." He walked out from behind the bar with a tray filled with glasses. "I tried to fluff her hair because trust me, sweetie, it needed it. She swatted at me, I might have swatted back a little too hard, and we both ended up going into the pool."

I closed my eyes for a moment. "Good thing she turned out to be the bad guy."

Kate took the glass of red punch Fern handed her. "If the girl didn't have skin issues, we might never have caught her."

"Here's to catching bad guys," Fern said after we all had a glass. "And pulling off fabulous weddings while doing it."

We all raised our glasses and drank.

"Look at the bright side, Annabelle." Kate winked at me. "Our next wedding can't be more of a disaster than this one."

I looked around desperately for some wood to touch, but there was none.

"You'd better hope not, since your wedding is coming up," Fern reminded her with a smug smile.

Kate's cheeks flushed, and she gave a nervous laugh. She'd been engaged to Daniel Reese, Mike's big brother, for a few months now, but hadn't made much progress with wedding planning, unless you counted deciding she wanted us to all fly down to Mexico for her last hurrah as a single woman. "That's right, but not before my bachelorette weekend."

"Why do I have a feeling her bachelorette weekend isn't going to be a low-key event?" Richard said to me with a tortured sigh.

"Because it's Kate, and because Fern is planning it," I told him.

He looked at both of them and shuddered. "Heaven preserve us."

Fern joined us holding his own glass of punch. "You have nothing to worry about. It will just be some sun, some pampering, and a touch of Tequila Mockingbird."

Richard rolled his eyes at Fern's drag name. "Please tell me this trip south of the border isn't just so your name will fit with the local cocktails."

Fern winked at him. "When in Rome. Or on the Riviera Maya."

My phone trilled, and I pulled it from my pocket and glanced down, both excited and nervous, when I saw my hunky husband's photo flash onto the screen.

"Does your hot cop hubbie know about what happened today?" Kate asked, peering at the screen.

"Not all of it," I admitted, answering the phone and putting it to my ear, a small rush going through me when I heard the deep rumble of his voice.

"Hey, babe."

"Hey, back," I said. "You're not going to believe what happened at the wedding."

He chuckled and let out a sigh. "Please don't tell me someone was murdered after all."

"Conga line!" Fern cried, tossing back the rest of his drink and pulling a reluctant Richard to his feet.

I laughed. "Well, no, but the night is young."

EPILOGUE

"Home at last," Kate said, as we stumbled into my apartment and dropped our bags on the floor. "Or close enough."

Richard staggered in behind us with an armload of white linens, which he unceremoniously dumped next to our bags. "Remind me again why we had to carry the linens back in our luggage."

"I promised Party Settings that we'd have them back to them by Monday, and I couldn't trust the shipping from the Bahamas. You were the one who couldn't function properly if the linens didn't reach the floor."

He eyed me and then the pile of white fabric. "You're right. They were worth it, even if my clothes did get horribly crushed from having to wedge some of them into my bag."

"As fun as the Bahamas was, it's always nice to get home." I flopped on the couch, inhaling the lingering scent of pizza, a telltale sign that my husband had spent the weekend ordering in. Although I usually loved the savory aroma of our favorite combo of sausage and green peppers, today it made my stomach turn.

"I feel like we need a vacation from our vacation," Kate said, joining me on the yellow twill couch.

Richard held up a finger. "Working a wedding—even a vow renewal—is never a vacation."

Kate let her head loll onto the back of the couch as she kicked off her high heel sandals. "And we have another wedding this coming weekend. I guess there's no rest for the Wicken."

"Or the wicked," Richard muttered as he headed toward my kitchen. "I take it Reese is on duty?"

"He caught a pretty big case the night of our vow renewal. A home invasion at a ritzy house. It's the second one in as many weeks."

Kate sat up and glanced at my door. "A home invasion?"

Richard poked his head through the opening between the kitchen and living room. "I doubt a fourth-floor walkup in an old building is a prime target."

I swiveled my head to take in my comfortable furniture and stacks of wedding magazines and file folders littering the available surfaces. There wasn't anything worth stealing even if a burglar did make the trek up the stairs.

Letting out a long breath, I closed my eyes. The flight back to DC hadn't been arduous, but we'd been forced to fly through Miami, which was my least favorite airport. Then our connecting flight had been delayed, meaning it was almost dark outside.

"You aren't sleepy, are you?" Kate asked. "I thought we could go out for dinner since your hot hubby isn't here to steal you away."

The thought of getting back up and going out to a restaurant sent a wave of weariness through me, but I forced myself to sit up. "I guess we should eat. The cookies on the plane don't count as a meal."

"They certainly do *not.*" Richard emerged from the kitchen holding open a Styrofoam take-out container. "And there's nothing in your refrigerator, not that that's a shock." He wrinkled his nose as he stared down at the container. "Was this once fish, Annabelle?"

The smell of the spoiled fish wafted across the room. Instantly, my exhaustion was replaced with nausea. I pressed a hand to my mouth and bolted to my feet, dashing past Richard and barely making it to the bathroom in time before I lost my lunch—or in this case, airplane cookies.

I braced my hands on the side of the sink, grateful for the cool porcelain as I heaved in deep breaths.

Kate's head popped around the open doorframe. "You okay?"

"Fine," I said with a forced smile. "I think the craziness of the weekend and the long day of travel got to me, that's all. Maybe it was something I ate."

She nodded, but her eyes narrowed. "We all ate the same thing, which was not much."

Richard appeared next to Kate. "What's going on?"

I took a step back. "You don't have that fish with you, do you?"

He held up his palms. "I put it in the trash where it

rightfully belonged." His eyes widened. "Please don't tell me you caught a bug in the Bahamas. I do not have time to get sick."

Kate folded her arms over her chest. "Oh, it's not a bug."

Richard and I both looked at her for a beat, then she cocked an eyebrow and glanced at my stomach. Richard sucked in a sharp breath and slapped a hand over his mouth.

"Don't be silly," I said. "I can't be…" But as soon as I thought about it and did some mental calendar math, I realized that I could be. Another wave of nausea made me grip the sink tighter.

"This can't be happening," Richard muttered, shaking his head. "They haven't even been married a year. I'm not ready for this."

You and me both, I thought.

Kate grinned at me. "Why don't I pop out and get a test while Richard has a nervous breakdown?"

My best friend shot her a look. "I am not having a nervous breakdown. You know I despise overreactions. This isn't an overreaction. This is the proper reaction for a surprise pregnancy during wedding season." He heaved in a ragged breath. "I might need a paper bag."

She patted him on the back. "Uh huh. While I'm at it, I'll grab a paper bag." She winked at me. "And a bottle of bubbly. This deserves a celebration."

"Bubbly?" Richard nearly shrieked. "She can't drink champagne if she's pregnant." He put an arm around me and bustled me out of the bathroom while shooting a murderous look over his shoulder at Kate. "Clearly, I'm going to have to be much more involved if my future godchild has a chance of being normal."

"More involved in my life than you are already?" I asked, as Kate gave me a wicked grin and slipped out the front door.

"Of course." He propelled me to the couch, sitting me down and propping my feet on the coffee table. "No more running around like a crazy person." He leveled a finger at me. "And no more investigations."

Before I could argue, the door swung open, and my downstairs neighbor Leatrice rushed in carrying Richard's Yorkie Hermès under one arm. Both were dressed in pajamas embellished in ice cream cones, and the octogenarian's jet-black hair was topped with a matching sleeping cap.

"I just heard." She gaped at me, her brightly lipsticked mouth open in obvious shock.

"How did you hear?" I asked, since my husband didn't even know. Then I shook my head, remembering her fondness for spy gear. If she'd installed listening devices in my place, I didn't want to know.

"Kate," she said before I could stop her. "She was on the phone to Fern as she passed my apartment."

If the news got back to my husband before I even took a proper test, heads were going to roll.

Richard placed at hand to his throat as he stared at Leatrice and his dog in their matching outfits. "Oh, good heavens. I know who is *not* going to oversee maternity wear."

Leatrice put a wriggling Hermès on the ground, and he scampered over to Richard, bells on his dog pajamas jingling. Richard picked him up and walked him to the kitchen, muttering to the little dog about trends versus fashion.

Leatrice sat next to me on the couch. "Don't you worry about a thing, dear. You've got a built-in babysitter in me. Just look at what a good job I do watching Hermès."

I sighed, wondering if there were a lot of giant onesies in her future.

When my phone buzzed, I pulled it out of my pocket, cringing when I saw that it was my husband. The news couldn't have traveled that fast, could it?

I answered and tried to make my voice sound normal. "Hey you."

"Hey, babe," he said. "You home yet?"

"Just got in." I let out a breath. Obviously, he hadn't heard.

"Sorry I didn't leave much in the fridge. I've been so busy I didn't manage to shop."

"It's fine. I didn't expect you to have time to get groceries."

"Is that Reese?" Richard poked his head through the divider. "Tell the daddy-to-be that he's forgiven, and Richard is on the case."

I held my breath, hoping that Mike hadn't heard him.

"Um, babe?" he asked after a long pause. "What did Richard call me?"

"You know how we talked about having kids in a year or two?" I took a quick breath and barreled on. "What would you think about speeding up that timeline?"

He was quiet for a moment. "I love that idea almost as much as I love you."

My throat tightened, and I blinked away tears. "Then you're going to love what I have to tell you next."

———

Thank you for reading *Jewel of the Aisle!*

This book has been edited and proofed, but typos are like little gremlins that like to sneak in when we're not looking. If you spot a typo, please report it to: laura@lauradurham.com
Thank you!!

ALSO BY LAURA DURHAM

Annabelle Archer Series:

Better Off Wed

For Better Or Hearse

Dead Ringer

Review To A Kill

Death On The Aisle

Night of the Living Wed

Eat, Prey, Love

Groomed For Murder

Wed or Alive

To Love and To Perish

Marry & Bright

The Truffle with Weddings

Irish Aisles are Smiling

Godfather of Bride

Claus for Celebration

Bride or Die

Slay Bells Ring

Jewel of the Aisle

*Annabelle Archer Collection: Books 1-4

Annabelle Archer Books available as Audiobooks:

Better Off Wed

For Better Or Hearse

Dead Ringer

Review to a Kill

Annabelle Archer Collection: Books 1-4

———

To get notices whenever I release a new book, follow me on BookBub:

ABOUT THE AUTHOR

Laura Durham has been writing for as long as she can remember and has been plotting murders since she began planning weddings over twenty years ago in Washington, DC. Her first novel, BETTER OFF WED, won the Agatha Award for Best First Novel.

When she isn't writing or wrangling brides, Laura loves traveling with her family, standup paddling, perfecting the perfect brownie recipe, and reading obsessively.

Find her on:
www.lauradurham.com
laura@lauradurham.com

Printed in Great Britain
by Amazon